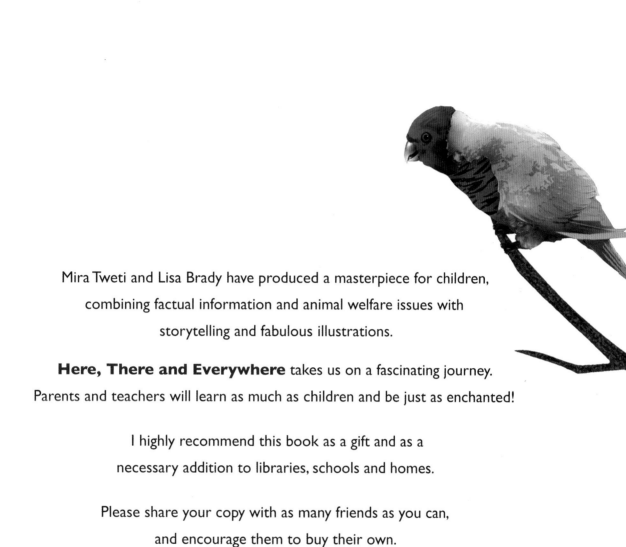

Mira Tweti and Lisa Brady have produced a masterpiece for children,
combining factual information and animal welfare issues with
storytelling and fabulous illustrations.

Here, There and Everywhere takes us on a fascinating journey.
Parents and teachers will learn as much as children and be just as enchanted!

I highly recommend this book as a gift and as a
necessary addition to libraries, schools and homes.

Please share your copy with as many friends as you can,
and encourage them to buy their own.

— DR. JANE GOODALL, DBE

ACKNOWLEDGMENTS

HERE, THERE AND EVERYWHERE WAS CREATED as a labor of love by a like-minded "dream team" that came together willing to help as needed and without funding or remuneration. None, save for the author, had any previous connections to parrots, but all donated considerable time, materials and talent for their betterment, and are thanked and commended for it.

All the *fabulous* illustrations are by the *fabulously* talented artist Lisa Brady. Thank you, Lisa! Far as I'm concerned, finding you proves that karma is at work in the world. You were clearly meant for *Sreeeeeeeet*, and *Sreeeeeeeet* for you!

The epitome of a great editor, Randy McCarthy, of The News Tribune of Tacoma, Washington, generously bestowed his excellent eye, journalistic experience and personal time to the words and ideas contained on these pages. It's always a pleasure to work with you and a privilege to be your colleague and friend. Deepest thanks doesn't nearly suffice. The truth is…I could not have done this without your help.

The style and design of each page reflects the talent of designer Ashlee Goodwin, founder of Fleuron Press (www.FleuronPress. com). We found her in the nick of time. She joined our collective and donated her labor without hesitation and on a moment's notice. We couldn't have afforded her otherwise and she enabled us to make our first printing deadline. Lisa and I are incredibly grateful to have her talent included here.

Many thanks to our printer, Craig Landers and the team at Taylor Specialty Books, for their stellar work in the production of this book.

Our exceptionally inspired Web site design was created by the talented Edward Good (www.frontlinegrafix.com). We were lucky to find someone who took *Sreeeeeeeet* to heart and brought him to life so beautifully. Thanks Edward, we're so glad to have you on the team!

Our gratitude goes out to the Jane Goodall Institute (www.JaneGoodall.org) and the Humane Society of the United States (www.hsus.org), two worthy animal welfare organizations whose support has been incalculable. They would love to hear from you and so would I!

Today, many books printed in the United States and Asia for the American market use Indonesian rainforest trees, the kind parrots depend on to live, or other limited natural resources. In an era of global warming and rampant deforestation, it is both reckless and irresponsible to destroy rapidly diminishing wildlife habitat for consumer products!

Though short on production funds, **Here, There and Everywhere** was determined not to contribute to this crisis. To this end, the project found an angel in Carolyn Moran at Living Tree Paper (www.livingtreepaper.com). Thanks to her, the book you are holding, which required thousands of huge sheets of paper, was printed on Living Tree's beautiful Déjà vu coated gloss text stock. The paper is made from 10% flax fiber, 40% recycled post consumer waste and 50% sustainably harvested trees certified by the Forest Stewardship Council.

As consumers it's important to remember that the chain of environmental destruction or repair starts and ends with us! Always check for a green indicator before you purchase.

Mira Tweti, Los Angeles, California, 2007
HereThereAndEverywhere@ParrotPress.org

PHOTO CREDITS

Images for the Indonesian Parrot Project were supplied by their directors, Stewart Metz and Bonnie Zimmerman, and are all ©the Indonesian Parrot Project. Many thanks to Hugh Choi for the photos of his free-flight Red-fronted Amazon(s) on the "About Parrots" page. For more of his great shots, go to www.ParrotPress.org.

It's hard to find a better photographer than Ron Batzdorf. The flattering image of me with ZaZu that Lisa Brady cartoonized in the biographical section is one of his.

Library of Congress txu 1-338-183 by Mira Tweti, Parrot Press Publishing.
ISBN 13: 978-0-615-17122-7

Published by

PARROT PRESS

California, January 2008

MANGO

ZAZU

FOR MANGO AND ZAZU WITH LOVE AND APPRECIATION…

Here, There and Everywhere is dedicated to my muse, Mango, the Rainbow lorikeet who inspired this story.

I wished for years to return Mango to his ancestral home in the rainforest of New Guinea. That is where his family lived before they were trapped for the pet trade and brought to the United States in the 1980s.

After we spent a decade together Mango died. Several parrot rescuers called me, offering condolences and lories to adopt. When I realized how many homeless lories there were, I worked to find them excellent, and permanent, living situations.

I consider that ongoing endeavor, and this book, part of Mango's legacy.

To date 45 birds—19 lorikeets (including two Moluccan-reds and a Black-capped), 21 Amazon parrots, four macaws and three ducks—are living in zoo exhibits, large aviaries in sanctuaries, or, in the case of the ducks, private homes with large yards to run.

The lories spend their days outdoors, flying and playing in trees, streams or waterfalls and, best of all, getting to live each day and roost each night within a flock.

Mango's sweet successor, ZaZu, had big shoes to fill when he came from Tennessee to live with me. He has done so admirably and with great finesse. This book is also dedicated to him and especially to Gina, Brandon, Amayla and Jaryn Knight for urging me to adopt him, and for their extraordinary friendship. Our families will be bound forever by the love of a lorikeet.

— *Mira*

FOREWORD
by DR. JANE GOODALL

WHEN I WAS ABOUT 8 YEARS OLD

I fell in love with Polynesia, the parrot who belonged to Doctor Doolittle. She taught him to understand the languages of all the animals — something I desperately wanted to be able to do myself! Back then, we didn't think about the cruelty involved in taking young parrots from the wild, away from their parents, their flock and their home. We didn't appreciate the suffering.

I have always hated birds in cages. In so many parts of Africa people keep parrots shut into small cages or perched on stands with their wing feathers cut, never able to fly. They are usually alone, too — because it is said they learn to talk better if they hear only human voices and have only humans for company. They are serving life sentences in solitary confinement, even though they have committed no crime, and seldom getting the constant attention they crave.

Many people buy a parrot with the best intentions, but most gradually spend less and less time with their pets. Their parrots may become sad, morose, pull out their feathers and sometimes become bad tempered and dangerous. Luckily, however, more and more sanctuaries are being set up to care for unwanted pets, and many more people understand it is usually a very bad thing to buy any wild animal for a pet. That is especially true of parrots, because they live so long and need so much attention. Even those born in captivity will be unhappy unless they can be part of a flock, or bond with a human with whom they can spend most of every day.

People owning parrots have often commented on their obvious intelligence, and were sure their birds knew what they were saying. Recently, a Caledonian crow proved, once and for all, that birds, despite their different kind of brain, can indeed work out complex problems by thinking things through. After that scientists had to admit that if crows had such clever minds, then obviously parrots did also! In fact, just as chimpanzees and other apes can learn sign language and use it to communicate with each other as well as their teacher, so, too, can parrots learn to understand the meaning of words.

In **Here, There and Everywhere**, we can feel, through the experiences of its hero, *Sreeeeeeeet*, the excitement and joy of learning to fly, taking showers in the rain, feeding, grooming and playing with his family and friends. And we share his anguish

when he is cruelly snatched away, imprisoned and misunderstood.

I shall never forget the first time I saw a flock of parrots flying overhead when I was being paddled along a river in the rain forest in Congo-Brazzaville. They were calling out to each other and moving through the air so fast, so joyously. That made me feel even sadder for the poor captives, deprived forever of the chance to fly freely through the forest. The mastery of the air is the gift they are born with.

— *Dr. Jane Goodall, DBE, is the founder of the Jane Goodall Institute and a United Nations Messenger of Peace.*

ON THE FAR SIDE OF THE WORLD, on the island of new Guinea, lived a young rainbow lorikeet parrot. He named himself *Sreeeeeeeet* so his father and mother *Kreeeeeeeet* and *Dreeeeeeeet*, could tell his call from his sister *Mreeeeeeeet's*.

Several times a day *Sreeeeeeeet's* parents flew to get sweet flower nectar to feed their young. As they returned to their nesthole in a dead tree, they called to let *Sreeeeeeeet* and *Mreeeeeeeet* know they were near. "*Sreeeeeeeet Mreeeeeeeet Kreeeeeeeet*," his father called.

When *Sreeeeeeeet* and *Mreeeeeeeet* heard their names, they knew they were being called, when they heard their father's name they knew he was the one calling. This is a way parrots know who is talking to them when other parrots are around. Their mother *Dreeeeeeeet* did the same. "*Dreeeeeeeet Kreeeeeeeet Sreeeeeeeet!*" *Sreeeeeeeet* squawked back.

"*Dreeeeeeeet Kreeeeeeeet Mreeeeeeeet!*" called *Mreeeeeeeet* excitedly. They both loved nectar and couldn't wait to be fed beak to beak!

The parrots were so loud they could be heard
here, there and everywhere throughout the rainforest.

Their squawks scared the tree kangaroo and the
spotted chital deer. And the rabbit-eared bandicoots
had to cover their sensitive ears.

The young birds ate a lot, and after they ate they pooped.
They took two steps back, pooped and took two steps forward.
They did the two-step here, then there and soon they had
pooped everywhere!

You might think their nest was messy and stinky, but it wasn't.
Insects were the parrots' cleaning crew. They loved the digested
fruit and flowers and gobbled it all up like little vacuum cleaners.

From their safe tree hole *Sreeeeeeeet* and *Mreeeeeeeet* watched the forest and learned about their world. They had no end of exciting and interesting things to see.

Sreeeeeeeet thought it was most fun to watch his flock as they flew high in the sky, performing acrobatic feats, or as they played in the trees, dangling by their feet.

Sreeeeeeeet yearned to fly with them. But his wing feathers hadn't grown in and his wings weren't strong enough to keep him aloft.

Finally, the day came when he felt ready to fly. He perched
outside the tree hole and fanned his colorful wings. His heart
raced as he flapped faster and faster and was lifted into the air.

His parents proudly watched as *Sreeeeeeeet* soared above
the tallest trees. He knew then that flying was what he
was meant to do!

He loved the feel of the sun on his back and the wind under his wings.

Sreeeeeeeet flew here, there and everywhere and grew very tired. He landed to rest and found he was lost! He'd never been out of the tree hole before and this part of the forest was unfamiliar to the little parrot.

He started to panic, squawking his name loud and fast: "*SREEEEEEEET SREEEEEEEET! SREEEEEEEET SREEEEEEEET!*"

His parents heard his alarm and calmly called back their names with his. "*Sreeeeeeeet Kreeeeeeeet,*" his father said. "*Sreeeeeeeet Dreeeeeeeet,*" his mother squawked. Hearing them he was reassured. He flew all the way home on the sound of their voices.

Once *Sreeeeeeeet* could fly he never wanted to land. He didn't care whether it was rainy or sunny, windy or cold.

Flying was freedom!

Sreeeeeeeet also loved that he was never alone. The flock always surrounded him in flight and on the ground like a traveling home.

Every day the parrots flew here, there and everywhere to eat flower pollen and nectar, tropical fruits and berries.

Sreeeeeeeet licked the inside of each bloom with the brush-like bristles on the tip of his tongue. It was like licking a lollipop. The bristles kept the powdery pollen from falling off and pollinated the flowers as he moved from one to another.

When *Sreeeeeeeet* traveled he pooped on the flowers and leaves, bushes and bees. His poop plopped seeds to the ground and they sprouted into new plants, trees and flowers.

The bees didn't mind the poop. They thought it tasted delicious! Insects and animals on the ground that couldn't climb as high as *Sreeeeeeeet* could fly liked the poop because it delivered nutritious foods they couldn't reach otherwise. All in all, the forest grew greener because *Sreeeeeeeet* and the other lorikeets lived there.

After the parrots ate, they bathed in the stream. They flapped their wings to wash them, splashing water here, there and everywhere!

After their baths the parrots relaxed. They played and preened each other as their feathers dried in the afternoon sun.

At night *Sreeeeeeeet* and his family roosted with the flock. He felt warm and safe in the midst of so many parrots that loved him.

While the flock slept, older sentinel lorikeets kept a lookout for any threats. But there were predators in the hills the parrots couldn't protect against…

One night poachers put up nets to trap the lorikeets.

The next day *Sreeeeeeeet* was flying from flower to flower when he was snagged. Frightened, he alerted the flock by squawking his name loudly over and over, "*SREEEEEEEET SREEEEEEEET!*" he squawked, "*SREEEEEEEET SREEEEEEEET!*" Any parrot that heard him was to come and help right away.

His parents came quickly, flying in circles over the poachers' heads to scare them off with their noisy squawks and bright colors. But the men just watched, hoping to trap them too.

Sreeeeeeeet's parents were frightened, but they had to rescue their son.

Bravely, they landed and walked carefully to avoid the traps. They got to *Sreeeeeeeet* and tried to free him. But the net was too thick for their little beaks to bite through.

They stayed as long as they could, dodging the trappers' nets. When the sun went down they had to flee because parrots can't see in the dark and the men could easily have grabbed them.

At dawn they flew back, but *Sreeeeeeeet* was gone. Frantically they called his name with their own so he would know they were searching for him. "*Sreeeeeeeet, Kreeeeeeeet!*" squawked his father. "*Sreeeeeeeet, Dreeeeeeeet!*" called his mother. Their calls echoed through the forest but *Sreeeeeeeet* didn't hear them. He was already too far away.

The men carried the trapped parrots out of the deep forest in wooden crates. *Sreeeeeeeet* and the other lories were crammed together. It was very hot and hard for them to breathe. Some felt sick. At the edge of the forest the poachers loaded the birds onto a truck and drove away.

When the truck started moving *Sreeeeeeeet* was so frightened he squawked even louder. "*SREEEEEEEET SREEEEEEEET!*" His parents heard him and called back. "*SREEEEEEEET KREEEEEEEET,*" his father squawked. "*SREEEEEEEET DREEEEEEEET,*" his mother called.

They flew after the truck but couldn't keep up. Their calls got softer and softer, "*Sreeeeeeeet, Sreeeeeeeet, Sreeeeeeeet, Sreeeeeeeet,*" as they fell behind. They watched the truck take *Sreeeeeeeet* away and it broke their hearts. *Sreeeeeeeet* saw them hovering, smaller and smaller, in the distance. *"I've lost my family, my flock and my forest. I am lost from my world,"* *Sreeeeeeeet* thought. He started to cry.

The lush forest became a dry dirt road. Giant tree trunks lay exposed on the ground, the sun blazing down on them. This once mighty forest had held rainwater in its roots, keeping the soil moist even in the driest times. In monsoon rains, the trees kept the howling winds at bay and prevented landslides by holding the ground in place. In the heat of summer, the forest shaded the earth and kept it cool. Now the trees were gone and the land was flat, empty, and baked by the sun.

Some forest species, like the lorikeets, had been there for more than a million years. Now their homes were torn down and trucked to factories where they were turned into pulp for toilet paper, books and magazines. Their land would grow food for people, not for them.

Sreeeeeeeet and the other parrots had never seen a place like this and it frightened them. The shrill screeches of chain saws wounding tree trunks hurt their ears and drowned out their squawks. And the thick dust of shavings burnt their eyes.

Worried, *Sreeeeeeeet* and the other parrots watched and wondered, *"Will we ever again fly here, there and everywhere?"*

After a while the road became a town. It all looked alien to the little birds.

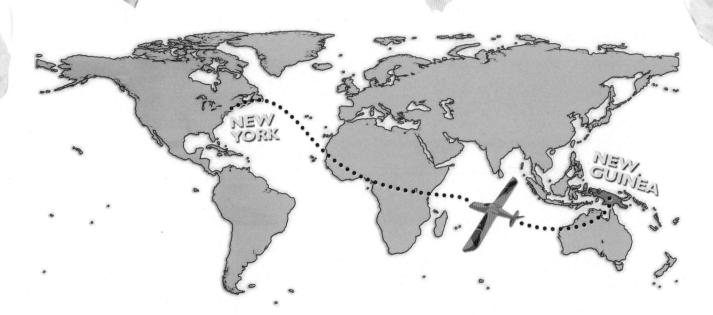

After a long ride on a plane and then in another truck Sreeeeeeeet was put in a cage in a pet store. He was very dirty and very tired. The food he was given wasn't the sweet nectar he needed, so he was hungry, too.

The store owner looked at him and shook his head.

"We'll have to get you spruced up," he said. "No one will want you like that."

He gave Sreeeeeeeet a bowl of water and some food. Sreeeeeeeet drank some and took a bath in the rest. It was nothing like his stream but it was all there was.

Each day Sreeeeeeeet squawked for his flock, "Sreeeeeeeet, Sreeeeeeeet," he called, hoping they would hear him and come. But they never did.

"You're a pretty bird, but you're a noisy one," the owner told Sreeeeeeeet. "You better stop all that racket, or no one will buy you and I'll be out a lot of money. You weren't cheap you know."

Sreeeeeeeet couldn't understand him, so he just kept squawking. He hoped the man would squawk back his name like parrots do when they get to know each other. "Sreeeeeeeet Sreeeeeeeet, Sreeeeeeeet Sreeeeeeeet," he said to start the conversation. But the owner thought parrots weren't smart and didn't realize Sreeeeeeeet was trying to speak with him.

Because of Sreeeeeeeet, the other animals in the store started making noise too. It took the owner an hour to quiet them down one by one.

Sreeeeeeeet hated being in a cage but when he was free he kept hitting the store window trying to fly home. He was confused about glass; in the rainforest, if you can see through something you can fly through it too. Sreeeeeeeet would hit the glass hard and fall to the floor so the owner kept him locked in his cage. One day Sreeeeeeeet started squawking loudly to be let out. The rest of the animals started barking and honking and screeching, too!

The store owner was trying to calm *Sreeeeeeeet* when the Smith family came in. The little boy was named Peter. He was 9. His parents had promised him any pet he wanted as a reward if he did well in school. He had gotten all A's and he was excited to choose.

There were so many animals — dogs, cats, parrots, a duck and even a monkey. But when Peter spotted *Sreeeeeeeet* he felt like he was looking at the most beautiful creature in the world.

"I want this bird," said Peter.

"It's too loud," said Peter's dad. "Listen to him squawking!"

"And aren't parrots messy?" asked Peter's mom.

"Well, that's true," the owner said.

But Peter responded quickly, "I'll make sure he stays in the cage all the time."

"It's not good for a bird to be in a cage all the time," said the owner. "They need to stretch their wings and move around freely like my birds do here."

"It's not good for me or my expensive furniture if he poops on it!" Peter's mom replied.

She suggested Peter pick another pet. But he insisted, and since they'd made a promise they bought *Sreeeeeeeet* and took him home.

The family lived in a posh apartment overlooking Central Park in New York City. Peter decided to call *Sreeeeeeeet* "Ripley."

Sreeeeeeeet didn't respond to the new name. You can't just rename a parrot if he likes the name he has.

Sreeeeeeeet kept trying to tell Peter who he was. He squawked that his name was *Sreeeeeeeet*, and that he'd been taken here, there and everywhere. He said he needed to go home to his trees, where the flowers, nectar, streams, and other lorikeets were waiting.

"*Sreeeeeeeet Sreeeeeeeet, Sreeeeeeeet Sreeeeeeeet,*" he said to start the conversation. He waited for Peter to respond. He thought Peter would squawk back his name like parrots do.

But Peter didn't understand lorikeet language, so he didn't say anything. *Sreeeeeeeet* thought Peter didn't hear him, so he squawked louder. "*SREEEEEEEET SREEEEEEEET! SREEEEEEEET SREEEEEEEET!*" he said.

Peter's parents told him to make *Sreeeeeeeet* stop. But you can't make a parrot stop squawking if that's what he wants to do.

Sreeeeeeeet never did learn Peter's name and Peter never learned *Sreeeeeeeet's*.

Sreeeeeeeet's squawking caused a lot of problems for the Smith family and their neighbors complained too!

As time went on, Peter thought *Sreeeeeeeet* was very happy in his cage because *Sreeeeeeeet* was always excited when he came into the room.

But *Sreeeeeeeet* got excited only when he saw Peter. The rest of the time he was very lonely. For a parrot free in the forest every day is new, different, and exciting. In a cage every day is the same, nothing changes.

One day Peter heard *Sreeeeeeeet* moaning sadly and finally understood.

"How would I like to be in a cage all day?" Peter thought to himself. He quickly realized how terrible a life that would be and set *Sreeeeeeeet* free.

"I'll fly back to my forest now," Sreeeeeeeet thought. He flew down the long hallway to the living room, looking for a way out.

But there were walls and windows here, there and everywhere. It was all strange to *Sreeeeeeeet* because there are no walls in the forest.

Peter's mom saw him heading for her white furniture and tried to catch him. But he didn't want to be trapped again so he flew away pooping all over everything!

Unlike the forest, there were no insects to clean up so the poop made a big mess. By the time Peter's father finally caught *Sreeeeeeeet* in a towel there was poop here, there and everywhere.

"That bird has got to stay in his cage!" he ordered Peter.

Before getting *Sreeeeeeeet*, Peter had never thought about the needs or wishes of a parrot. He had no idea they needed so many things besides food and a cage.

Now knowing how hard it was on *Sreeeeeeeet* to be confined, Peter sometimes sneaked him out when the bedroom door

was closed. And *Sreeeeeeeet* squawked a lot less when he did.

Peter was finally seeing *Sreeeeeeeet* as an individual just like him and not as a pet with pretty feathers and a beak. He learned *Sreeeeeeeet* needed a lot of the same things he did—like playing, bathing, and most of all having someone to spend time with.

Sreeeeeeeet started to love Peter. He liked having his tummy tickled and giggled when Peter did it. And he liked to hear Peter laugh. *Sreeeeeeeet* figured it was as close to a squawk as Peter could get.

Each morning, like many parrots do, *Sreeeeeeeet* squawked to welcome the sunrise. "*Sreeeeeeeet Sreeeeeeeet*," he called to the sun.

And every morning he woke Peter's parents when he did. To get back to sleep, they had to cover their ears just like the rabbit-eared bandicoots in the forest.

Peter tried to stop *Sreeeeeeeet's* squawking by covering his cage with a blanket. But it reminded *Sreeeeeeeet* of the trappers' net. He got so frightened he squawked even louder, "*SREEEEEEEET SREEEEEEEET! SREEEEEEEET SREEEEEEEET!*"

Sreeeeeeeet heard the city noises, the car horns and sirens, on the busy street below. He squawked, "*Sreeeeeeeet Sreeeeeeeet*," to these strange jungle sounds, still hoping his flock was out there and would rescue him. But they never answered.

The longer Peter had *Sreeeeeeeet* the less time he spent with him and the more time he spent with his friends. After a year, Peter just said "Hi" and "Bye" to *Sreeeeeeeet* when he came and left. *Sreeeeeeeet* was left alone in Peter's room most of the time.

Sreeeeeeeet tried talking to the pigeons on the window ledge for company. "*Sreeeeeeeet Sreeeeeeeet*," he called, but they just looked at him strangely. Like people in different countries, birds of different species speak different languages.

Parrots live long and they never forget the beings they care for. To *Sreeeeeeeet*, the world was bleak without his flock and family, and now, without Peter's companionship. He got so sad, he started pulling out his feathers.

One day, the Smiths had a party for some important people. When they introduced Peter a loud man in a toupee said, "I hear you've got a parrot!"

"Yes," said Peter.

"Can we see him?" asked a woman in a fancy red dress.

"Sure," said Peter without thinking.

When Peter came back with *Sreeeeeeeet* on his shoulder the loud man tried to pet him. *Sreeeeeeeet* found it very rude for a strange person to touch him and bit him hard!

"OWWW!" the loud man yelled at *Sreeeeeeeet.*

The little bird got scared and took off. He flew here, there and everywhere around the living room. And, as you might guess, everywhere he flew he pooped! First he pooped on the man's toupee and then on the lady's fancy red dress. And, of course, he pooped all over the nice white furniture. (Peter's mom had to get it professionally cleaned after the last time.)

"Yuck!" yelled the woman in the fancy red dress.

Without thinking the loud man grabbed the poopy toupee off his head and everyone at the party saw his secret: He had fake hair hiding his hairless head.

While they stared at the man, *Sreeeeeeeet* found an open window in the kitchen and flew out.

"I'll fly back to my flock now," *Sreeeeeeeet* thought and started calling for his parents, *"Sreeeeeeeet Kreeeeeeeet; Sreeeeeeeet Dreeeeeeeet."* But, of course, there was no answer because he was the only wild lorikeet flying in New York.

The city street was full of big buses, honking cars and boys zipping by on bicycles. It scared the little bird, so he flew to the mass of trees in front of him.

"There's a parrot in Central Park," someone yelled as *Sreeeeeeeet* flew by. Peter, who had run out to catch him, heard and followed.

Everyone was dazzled at *Sreeeeeeeet's* colors as he whizzed over their heads like a bullet! Peter marveled at *Sreeeeeeeet* soaring through the sky. *Sreeeeeeeet's* heart beat fast. He didn't know how much he missed flying until he was in the air again.

Peter realized then that *Sreeeeeeeet* could never be owned. He could only be kept from living his real life.

Soon *Sreeeeeeeet* felt lost and tired from flying around this strange place that had trees but wasn't a forest and was cold compared to his warm tropical island.

He tried to land but a big dog barked and chased after him. He was relieved when he saw Peter running toward him. He flew to Peter's shoulder and clung there until he was back in his cage.

Getting the furniture professionally cleaned twice cost more than buying *Sreeeeeeeet*, so

Peter's parents decided it was time for him to go back to the pet store.

Peter maintained good grades in school that year by writing stories about Sreeeeeeeet and what the parrot had taught him. He convinced his parents that money wasn't the most important thing. Sreeeeeeeet's happiness was.

He said they all had to be responsible for Sreeeeeeeet's future, since that's what they had really purchased that day at the pet store.

Mr. and Mrs. Smith saw that their son was right and agreed with him. They realized then that he hadn't just gotten good grades, he had earned them by learning, and had grown mature in the process.

Peter had an idea and together the family worked on it. First, they bought books on lorikeets to know more about them.

Then they contacted experts like ornithologists (bird scientists) and avian veterinarians (bird doctors) and shared their idea: They wanted to take Sreeeeeeeet back to his rainforest.

It wouldn't be easy for them or for Sreeeeeeeet. He would have a lot of blood tests and exams. And they would need permission from the government of New Guinea. They all agreed it would be worth it for the little bird and for them, for they would have helped him get home.

Soon the day came and Peter opened *Sreeeeeeeet's* cage for the last time.

They put him in a carrier and then on a plane that flew here, there and everywhere to reach the other side of the world. It finally landed in New Guinea, the mountainous island country where *Sreeeeeeeet* was born. When they got off the plane the air smelled familiar to *Sreeeeeeeet*.

A government official and an avian veterinarian met them at the airport and drove them from the city toward the green mountains in the distance.

Peter let *Sreeeeeeeet* sit on his hand to see out the window. "Do you recognize this place?" he asked. *Sreeeeeeeet* did. It looked like home.

They watched the city turn into a village, then into an open road and finally into the forest.

At last they came to a preserve, an area where the trees couldn't be cut and would be protected forever.

They released *Sreeeeeeeet* into a large aviary with fruit trees and tropical flowers.

"He'll only be quarantined in here for a month," said the veterinarian. "Then he can go where he likes," said the official.

Peter smiled, knowing *Sreeeeeeeet* would be happy to hear that if only he understood English. But Peter was sad too, knowing it was the last time he would see *Sreeeeeeeet*.

As for *Sreeeeeeeet*, he was so happy to be back in his surroundings that he didn't think at all about Peter. He would later, and was grateful when he did.

It started to rain and *Sreeeeeeeet* squawked with joy when he felt the drops on his feathers. He flew up to a tree to take a shower, swinging from the highest branches.

Peter waved goodbye sadly as the green of *Sreeeeeeeet*'s feathers merged with the leaves of the tree.

A month later *Sreeeeeeeet* was free to go. The aviary door was left open and fresh food was put in, offering *Sreeeeeeeet* the option to stay where he would be safe.

Sreeeeeeeet knew being alone in the forest was dangerous. But he also knew it was better to try to find his wild life and fail, than be protected forever. So he took to the air.

The familiar feeling of the sun on his back and the wind under his wings made him elated and restored his spirit. He called out his name across the lush mountains, "*Sreeeeeeeet Sreeeeeeeet*," and in the steep valleys, "*Sreeeeeeeet Sreeeeeeeet*" so the flock would know he was back.

But there was no answer and he feared that trappers had gotten them, too!

That night he roosted alone on a tree branch. The full moon bathed him in light so he wasn't afraid. He cocked his head and stared at the glowing moon. It was as beautiful as he remembered it.

The next day he began his search again. "*Sreeeeeeeet Sreeeeeeeet,*" he squawked to the morning sun. But now, instead of silence, he heard many lorikeet voices calling him all at once. "*Sreeeeeeeet Mreeeeeeeet!*" squawked his sister. "*Sreeeeeeeet Dreeeeeeeet!*" squawked his mother. "*Sreeeeeeeet Kreeeeeeeet,*" squawked his father.

And then the whole flock circled around him, calling his name in a beautiful song. "*Sreeeeeeeet Sreeeeeeeet!*" they sang. "*Sreeeeeeeet Sreeeeeeeet! Sreeeeeeeet Sreeeeeeeet!*"

Sreeeeeeeet was so happy to hear their voices, he danced in the air!

His family and flock were so excited to see him they kept all the animals in the rainforest awake well into the night.

Once again Sreeeeeeeet was bathing in the rain, being preened by the other lories and eating sweet nectar. And, of course, he was pooping here, there and everywhere!

*When one journey ends
a new one always begins…*

Sreeeeeeeet soon met a beautiful lorikeet named *Treeeeeeeet*. The two traveled everywhere together.

That spring, the pair searched for a big hole in a dead tree to make their nest and raise their young. When they did, they had two, as all Rainbow lorikeets do.

One was a boy who called himself *Breeeeeeeet*. The other was a girl whose call was *Lreeeeeeeet*.

Just like his parents had done, *Sreeeeeeet* squawked their names and his, "*Breeeeeeeet Sreeeeeeeet; Lreeeeeeeet Sreeeeeeeeet*," to tell the chicks they were on the way home with delicious nectar to feed them beak to beak.

And once again, the rabbit-eared bandicoots had to cover their sensitive ears as the loud, but happy, squawks echoed through the rainforest, here, there and everywhere!

IN THESE NEXT PAGES you'll find interesting information on parrots in general and lories in particular, as well as the stories of two pet parrots now living in rescues after their owners gave them up. One of them, named Kirby, was caught in the wild like *Sreeeeeeeet* and hasn't seen his forest again.

You'll also find photos and information of parrots rescued from smugglers at the Indonesian Parrot Project!

Visit **Here, There and Everywhere** on the Web at **www.ParrotStory.com**

Which has parrot things to see, hear and do —

✦ *Sreeeeeeeet* animations!

✦ Listen to the loud squawks of a real flock of rainbow lorikeets!

✦ Join the Parrot of the Month Art Competition.

Every month two illustrations will be picked in the 4-to-6-year-old and 7-to-11-year-old age groups. The artists will be interviewed on their own Web page and they will win a free set of **Here, There and Everywhere** posters!

✦ Join one of our programs to sponsor a wild parrot or one living in captivity. Your parrot is waiting for you!

♦ You're My Parrot! sponsorship program: **You'll get to know a parrot personally and help a bird and a rescue at the same time. If you pick a rescue near you could even go visit your parrot!**

♦ Join the Wild Parrot Sponsorship program and pick a group of wild Rainbow lorikeets, cockatoos or other parrots confiscated from trappers that are now being cared for by the Indonesian Parrot Project on the island of Seram, not far from *Sreeeeeeeet's* home on New Guinea. Some of the parrots will be returned to their forest — maybe it'll be one of yours!

Sreeeeeeeet says "See you at the Web site!"

ABOUT PARROTS
by RICHARD FARINATO

PARROTS ARE THE STUFF OF DREAMS.

Almost any color you might imagine can be found among the more than 340 species of parrots living in the American, Asian, African and Oceana tropic (and some not-so-tropic) zones.

One type is about three inches long with soft pastel green and turquoise feathers; another is almost three feet long with feathers of primary red, yellow and blue, looking like a rainbow on the wing in flight.

Although we may identify them by names other than "parrot" (budgie, parakeet, lovebird, cockatoo, macaw, lory, conure and cockatiel), they are all, regardless of size and coloring, members of the parrot family (Psittacidae).

All share some common traits. One is a bill that is unmistakably hook-like; another is a pair of very talented feet. They also share long life spans, complex social interactions between birds and among flock members, high intelligence and great (though by no means melodious) vocal abilities, including mimicry.

Parrots lay two to four eggs in a nest, which generally contains little or no bedding. Though both sexes in some species might share incubation duties, in most cases the female does the sitting. The male feeds her during this period and in the first days after the chicks hatch. Later on, when the female begins to leave the nestlings for short periods of time to feed herself, both parents nourish the young.

Parrots feed their babies by pumping a rich, milky mixture of partially digested food into the youngster's wide-open bills. Devoted parents, they keep this up until their babies have grown out their feathers and left the nest. Even then, the family stays together while the babies learn the ins and outs of parrot life, which can be complicated.

Learned skills are critical for parrots, since they live very long lives: 50 to 70 years for the larger species and 15 to 20 for smaller types. The rigors of a life in the wild (predators, parasites and weather extremes) may shorten this span, but that doesn't mean a bird can ignore learning where the best trees are for feeding and sleeping, or where the mineral-rich cliffs are, or how to sound an alarm call when a hawk is spotted. The flock offers lots of models to follow, as well as providing the added protection of numbers.

Still, parrots worldwide are in trouble. The twin threats of lost habitat and encroaching humans added to the constant demand for these birds as pets have caused the disappearance of some species and the real risk of extinction for many more.

Since Roman times, the pet parrot has been a highly sought-after status symbol. Now, it's not just royalty that keeps a parrot.

Birds as a whole routinely show up as the third or fourth most popular choice in U.S. pet industry surveys. And though captive breeding might take some of the pressure off a wild species, the marketing of any animal in large numbers brings with it humane and ethical questions.

Excerpted from Parrots *by Richard Farinato, director of Captive Wildlife Programs and the Wildlife Advocacy Division of the Humane Society of the United States. You can read this article, "A Closer Look at Wildlife-Parrots" in its entirety at www.ParrotStory.com or at www.hsus.org.*

MORE ABOUT LORIKEETS

LORY PARROTS LIKE *Sreeeeeeeet* are called lorikeets for the same reason parakeets have "keet" at the end of their names: it means they have a long tail. Otherwise there's no difference between lory and lorikeet, and you can say either and be correct.

There are 56 species of lory parrots, ranging in color and size from the large Black lory to the small Tahiti blue lory.

Lories are found from as far north as the Philippines and as far south as Tasmania off the southeastern coast of Australia. In Australia, Rainbow lorikeets—which look similar to *Sreeeeeeeet* except that they have orange and yellow feathers on their tummies instead of black and red—are as common as pigeons! You can see—and hear—noisy flocks of them in parks and on streets in big cities such as Sydney and Melbourne. (You can listen to their loud, high-pitched squawks at **www.ParrotStory.com**.)

Rainbow lorikeets are brave and adventurous birds, and will fly in open kitchen windows, looking for food, and eat it if they find it — even if the people are home! A lot of people leave food for them just to watch these wonderfully colorful birds eat with their brushed tongues.

Lories range from coastal areas, like beaches where they hang out in coconut palms, to high in mountain forests. Some live in very hot and humid areas and others in cooler ones. This makes the birds very adaptable.

Australia has seven species of lories, Indonesia has 20 and New Guinea has more than any place else with 29. These three places are surrounded by water, and too far for lories to fly to on their own. So how did they end up so close but so far away from each other? People might have brought them by boat but there's another possibility.

In prehistoric times, the land mass of the three countries was united in a "supercontinent" called Gondwanaland. After it broke into different pieces (beginning 135 million to 65 million years ago) there was still a land-bridge and the lories might have spread out across it. When the rest of the land split into what is now Australia, the thousands of islands of Indonesia and the largest tropical island in the world, New Guinea, they were separated forever.

To learn more about lories, visit the World Parrot Trust at **www.parrots.org** and click on "All About Parrots." You'll find a section on them and a list of lory species, with photos and information about them a mile long! Have fun!

ABOUT HERE, THERE AND EVERYWHERE
AND HOW YOU CAN HELP PARROTS

FOR A LONG TIME, wild parrots like *Sreeeeeeeet* were trapped in forests around the world and sent to far-away countries to be sold as pets. Many are still here because, as the story says, parrots live long lives.

They don't get to fly or play in streams and trees with their flock. They can't choose a mate and raise a family. But they and all the baby birds they have hatched over the years make up the 50 million to 60 million parrots living in the United States today.

Like *Sreeeeeeeet*, most parrots squawk so loudly they would wake you and your neighbors! Rainbow lorikeets don't like to chew on wood very much, but bigger parrots love it. They find destroying furniture a lot of fun! All parrots poop here, there and everywhere, and they bite, too, when they feel like it.

Usually, people buy a parrot and only later learn these things. That causes lots of problems, for the owners and for the birds! The parrots can't help what they do; it's in their natures because they are wild animals. Still, most people don't want birds in their homes that do things meant for a jungle. But, unlike *Sreeeeeeeet*, very few are returned to their forest homes.

And that is where **Here, There and Everywhere** and the reality of pet parrots differ. Bringing a bird back to the rainforest, after it has lived as a pet for a while, is a long, expensive and complicated process, so it is rarely done. In the story, the Smith family returns *Sreeeeeeeet* to the forest to show you the wonderful and rich life he was meant to have being free.

Living alone in a cage is not good for a wild animal with a social nature, and parrots tell us so. About one in 10 pluck their feathers, something they don't do in the wild. And, if left alone too long, they scream and bite themselves or others. Unfortunately, the more they do that, the less they get to come out of their cages!

Most people don't know there are hundreds of rescues and sanctuaries just for pet parrots! They are filled with unwanted pet birds and every week, sometimes every day, owners call and ask them to take their parrots, too. The problem of unwanted parrots is a crisis, and many experts now say parrots should not be kept as pets at all.

It is a full-time job to care for the many birds the rescues and sanctuaries take in. While many are fine, others have behavior problems and need a lot of one-on-one attention, love and care. Some rescues struggle to keep their doors open because they depend on donations and the general public is unaware of this serious problem.

Here, There and Everywhere helps parrot rescues, the Indonesian Parrot Project and other animal welfare organizations through the Parrot Press Donation Program, which donates a percentage of the money raised from each book sold. But it is not enough.

COSTA AND BABY Costa is a Green-wing macaw and Baby is a Blue and gold macaw. They would not be a pair in the wild because they are different species. They bonded in captivity, because like *Sreeeeeeeet*, they were lonely alone. They live with other unwanted parrots at the Parrots First rescue in Burbank, California.

Wherever you live, there is an avian rescue not too far from you that needs support. If you are thinking of buying a parrot, don't! One is waiting for you at a rescue, so please check with them first.

You may be able to sponsor or foster a parrot, volunteer or raise money in your community to help them. They would love to hear from you even if it's just to say you read this book and appreciate the work they do! There is a list of rescues, with links and ways to donate on our Web site, below.

Parrot Press has made it easy to help a needy parrot! Just sign up for the *You're My Parrot!* Sponsorship Program. You'll see photos and biographies of rescue parrots available for Internet sponsorship. Keep coming back to see updates, notes from their caretakers and some day-in-the-life stories telling what it's like to run a parrot rescue!

Next are two stories of rescue parrots, Kirby, Cluckie and Jazz. They'll give you an idea of the kinds of birds you'll see and the kinds of lives they've had.

Here, There and Everywhere Web site:

www.ParrotStory.com

AVIAN RESCUE PARROT PROFILE: KIRBY

KIRBY
GREEN-WING MACAW

AGE **About 28**

LIFE EXPECTANCY **60 to 80 years**

NATIVE TO **South America**

INFORMATION SUPPLIED BY **Midwest Avian Adoption and Rescue Services (MAARS), Minneapolis, Minnesota**

KIRBY WAS CAPTURED and taken from his home in the rainforests of South America. He was separated from his flock and transported to a U.S. quarantine station, where he was held until he was released to the bird dealer who'd paid to have him captured. For the next 25 years, Kirby was passed from home to home, misunderstood and miserable. He came to MAARS terrified of humans.

At first, Kirby cowered in his cage and cried quietly, like a macaw chick would for her parents. The large red, green and blue bird with an enormously powerful beak was so afraid. Then, not long after joining the flock of other parrots, Kirby became interested in Apollo, a Blue and gold macaw.

Kirby made it clear he prefers not to see another human and would be most happy if he could spend the rest of his life among other macaws. After several months, he learned that the staff would give him all the space and time he needed. He decided it was best to keep things that way. He had learned over many years that aggression would keep a comfortable distance between himself and humans.

To honor his choices, MAARS is searching for an appropriate placement in a sanctuary where he can live outdoors with other birds and have minimal human contact. Unfortunately, because of limited space in such facilities, it might take years to find Kirby his permanent home among a flock.

CLUCKIE AND JAZZ

CLUCKIE
FEMALE QUAKER
(ALSO CALLED A "MONK" PARAKEET)

AGE 10

LIFE EXPECTANCY At least 30 years

NATIVE TO Central Bolivia and Southern Brazil
to Central Argentina

INFORMATION SUPPLIED BY Foster Parrots,
Rockland, Massachusetts

CLUCKIE WAS GIVEN to Foster Parrots in 2004. The rescue's staffers thought she would integrate happily into their small flock of quakers and find fulfillment building nests. They thought she'd be chatty and gregarious, as all quakers are. But that was not to be. Cluckie seemed to think she was above other quakers and refused to join the flock. She kept herself separate and behaved aggressively toward anyone who tried to approach. She was a loner.

Then Jazz arrived. The big, handsome mealy Amazon was introduced into the community about two months after Cluckie arrived. She took one look at him and knew he was the bird for her! She spent the first day trying to be with him. She sidled up to him, but he pushed her away with one big, gentle foot. Mealys are, by nature, gentle giants. Quakers, on the other hand, are bossy and relentless. By the next day Jazz had given in to the amorous demands of the pushy Cluckie and let himself be had. They are, by far, the oddest couple at Foster Parrots.

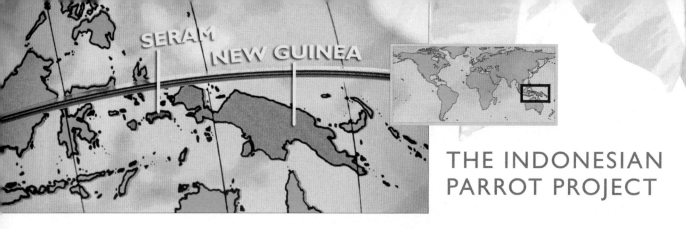

SERAM
NEW GUINEA

THE INDONESIAN PARROT PROJECT

THE INDONESIAN PARROT PROJECT is based on Seram, Indonesia, a small tropical island just below *Sreeeeeeeet's* island of New Guinea. The town is busy and noisy with children playing on the streets and swimming in the ocean.

The Parrot Project's Kembali Bebas rehabilitation center and sanctuary is in the forest and is very peaceful, aside from the squawking of 200 healthy parrots playing and socializing in the outdoor aviaries. These parrots weren't so healthy (or happy) when they first got there.

Trappers capture many kinds of lories and cockatoos in the forest. Like Peter, people want them for pets because of their colors and personalities. In Indonesia and New Guinea, some pet parrots are kept chained to a perch. Others are sold at dirty, crowded bird marts where thousands of parrots and other birds are kept in small cages.

When authorities arrest trappers and smugglers they confiscate the parrots and bring them to Kembali Bebas. The facility now has 200 parrots, including many lorikeet species. More come all the

time. When *Sreeeeeeet* arrived at the pet store he was dirty, hungry, tired and very scared. These parrots are too, terrified and traumatized from the violence of being trapped and confined.

At Kembali Bebas, the birds, surrounded by their forest and treated gently, soon realize they are safe, outdoors and with others like them. And there are facilities—such as a veterinary building and quarantine, plus a staff of 12 people who know a lot about parrots—to care for them.

The name Kembali Bebas means "Return to Freedom" in Indonesian. The first bird to be returned to freedom was a Rainbow lorikeet, like *Sreeeeeeeet*, that had been kept chained to a wooden perch

by its owner. That was four years ago. Since then staffers have helped more than 250 confiscated parrots, one quarter of them lories.

The Parrot Project ended trapping in a district on North Seram by employing all the parrot trappers there. Now they are parrot caretakers, working and being paid so that they don't need, or want, to trap birds any more.

The Parrot Project helps Indonesians realize their parrots and forests are the planet's priceless treasures and should be protected for future generations. To help villagers, members of the Parrot Project show them ways to make money besides selling birds.

On Seram, villagers collect kenari nuts, which are loved by cockatoos and other parrots. The villagers crack the hard shells by hand to get the nuts out and then ship them to the United States, where they are sold on the Parrot Project's Web site as "MoluccaNuts." Now parrots around the world can enjoy them and the residents of Seram have an income from something they can easily find but could not sell locally.

For 10 years, the Parrot Project has fought to protect parrots from the pet trade. Project members met with village elders and chiefs on the New Guinea islands of Gam and Batanta in Eastern Indonesia. The Parrot Project brings eco-tourists there, which helps the economy and gives villagers a reason to protect their wildlife. The Parrot Project also gave desks and other supplies for the schoolhouses. These desks say "a donation for bird conservation."

In return, Gam and Batanta residents promised to stop trapping. But Batanta has a lot of logging. It is impossible to protect parrots if their forests are being cut down.

YOU CAN HELP!

TO HELP LORIKEETS, cockatoos and other parrots trapped in Indonesia and New Guinea and to protect them in the rainforests:

Donate to the Indonesian Parrot Project by going to www.indonesian-parrot-project.org. One hundred percent of all funds goes directly to helping the birds.

Sponsor a wild parrot at the Parrot Project at www.ParrotStory.com and help your bird get the food and care it needs—and maybe see it returned to the forest! You'll also get regular updates—information, photos, video footage and blog entries—from the kids and staff at the Parrot Project!

Invite your friends to join you! Tell them the best place to keep a parrot is in a forest, not in a living room. They can join you in helping parrots stay in their trees!

AUTHOR & ILLUSTRATOR

MIRA TWETI is an award-winning investigative journalist whose articles have appeared in The Los Angeles Times, The New York Times, The Village Voice, The L.A. Weekly and numerous magazines.

Over the last nine years, she has written extensively about parrots, the pet bird trade and animal welfare issues and legislation. Her articles have helped pass four pieces of legislation to protect unweaned parrots and other animals in the pet industry. Her exposés on the parrot trade for The Los Angeles Times Magazine (*Plenty to Squawk About*) and The News Tribune of Tacoma, Washington, (*Parrots in Peril*) garnered Genesis awards from the Humane Society of the United States.

She has produced and directed a feature documentary about companion birds (*Birds of a Feather*) and is at work on another (*Little Miss Dewie: a Duckumentary*) about her and an orphaned Indian runner duck that lived in her Los Angeles apartment for two months while she searched for the perfect home. Mira is also the author of an investigative examination of the global parrot crisis titled *People v. Parrots: The Sometime's Funny, Always Fascinating, and often Catastrophic Collision of Two Intelligent Species*, to be published by Viking in 2008.

LISA BRADY was raised in an environment of art and nature amid a close family that nurtured the love of both. Her first teacher was her mother, an accomplished painter who worked from their New England home, and encouraged her daughter's talent. Lisa's father has also been a source of wisdom and strength throughout her life.

Lisa studied art at the L.W. Swank Studio in New Hampshire from the time she was 12 until she moved to Los Angeles at 17. Her desire to have her entire back tattooed led to a career as a tattoo artist. She and her husband, Tommy, opened their own business, TTR Studio, and built a steady following in Scotland. Her work was featured in such books as "Electric Tattooing by Women", "Endless Journeys" and "Arabic Tattoos."

In 2005, after seven years in the trade, she retired (still tattoo-less) after a change in spiritual beliefs. Since then she has focused on freelance art, commissioned portraits, storyboard layouts, conceptual art and other forms of illustration.

Lisa set out with the idea of illustrating a children's book but turned down many opportunities that proved meaningless. When she read *Here, There and Everywhere* the story swept her into its fold. An accomplished portraitist, Lisa was able to instill the vibrancy and sensitivity of real lorikeets into the book. Lisa lives in Los Angeles with her husband, an extraordinary musician and her best friend, without whose help these illustrations would never have existed; and their pug, Puggy.